ISBN-13: 978-0-8249-5629-5

Published by Ideals Children's Books
An imprint of Ideals Publications
A Guideposts Company
Nashville, Tennessee
www.idealsbooks.com

Library of Congress CIP data on file

Caseside and jacket printed in U.S.A.
Text printed and bound in Mexico

RRD-Rey_Dec10_1

Designed by Eve DeGrie

To my husband, Greg:
Life is a zoo, and I wouldn't have wanted
to share this life with any zookeeper but you.
Love always, always, always, Kathy

To my family, Lorien, Calvin, Sammy, Mattie, and Max,
who make our zoo a home. –G.F.

The View at the Zoo

Written by
Kathleen
Long Bostrom

Illustrated by
Guy Francis

ideals children's books.
Nashville, Tennessee

Rise and shine! Attention, please!
Monkeys, get down from those trees!

Wake your cubs up, Mrs. Bear!
Mr. Lion, comb that hair!

Elephant,
please wipe your nose.

Pink flamingos—
on your toes!

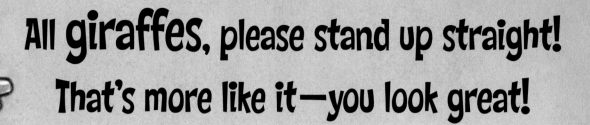

All **giraffes**, please stand up straight!
That's more like it—you look great!

All is ready.
Come on in!
Let the day of fun begin.

GIFT SHOP

My, what
silly things they do,
all these creatures
at the zoo.

Walking on all kinds of feet,
dancing to an inner beat.

Babies riding on their backs,
on their bellies, snug in sacks.

Hear the silly sounds they speak,
as they howl and squawk
and shriek!

How they eat! They never stop!
That one looks about to pop!

See them prance and
primp and preen,
trying to stay neat and clean.

Some of them are quite a fright!
Watch your fingers—
they may bite!

Sun is setting in the sky. Everybody, say goodbye!
Please go home so we can sleep—
time for us to count our sheep.

EXIT

Whew! They're leaving. Off they go!
They all put on quite a show!

What a hoot!
Folks have no clue
the view that WE have
at the zoo!

The End